T0274422

SHINE

Written by

RICK HALL

Illustrated by

Natalia Slattery

For my dad.
I understand now.

Little deer, little deer
the night is cold and I am all alone
the night is cold and I am all alone
all alone

Three weeks has passed since M'dad and Uncle Elvy went into the woods, and now M'dad's gettin' antsy. We know it's near time to go back in.

"It's the perfect night to go," says M'dad, in a hushed voice, cockin' his head as he pulls back the kitchen curtain and stares into the dark. The moon's covered with a cold mist, and we've just enough light to show us the way along the trail, but not so much it'll show our shadows on the hillside.

But Mother don't want us to go. "It's a school night," she says. And even though I missed the first two weeks of classes to help M'dad and Uncle Elvy get the corn outta the field, I was still able to catch up to the rest of the kids. "And wouldn't it be a shame," she says, "if you fell asleep durin' studies tomorrow."

Grandmother don't want us to go neither. She sits in the corner and spits a wad of tobacco into the coffee can on the

floor. Her rockin' gets faster as Mother makes a bigger fuss, 'til she cain't hold back no more. "The Devil's in that holler," starts up Grandmother. "Ain't no place for them boys!"

But before she can finish, Uncle Elvy cuts her short. "Aren't no Devil at'all," he says. "It's only Mr. Stevens, who'd just as soon shoot'cha as look at'cha." Uncle Elvy looks at me and Jack and Jerry, all serious. Then he winks and goes back to playin' cards.

"'Tis the Devil," says Mother, givin' M'dad her look. "And Mr. Stevens knows the Devil's come for his bottles."

"Uncle Elvy cain't go," says M'dad, "since he broke his leg fallin' outta the hay loft."

"And ain't it a shame it weren't his neck," says Mother, "instead of one of his little Irish bird legs."

Me, Jack, and Jerry laugh, but not like we always do when Mother cracks on Uncle Elvy. Cause none of us—me, Jack, nor Jerry—wants to go. We know it'll turn out the way it always turns out, and there'll be Hell to pay. But M'dad gives Mother the look and she shuts it, and tends to the dishes. That's that, and off we go to the barn to hitch up Old Nancy and load the bottles into the wagon, 'cause there'd be even more Hell to pay if we didn't.

*** *** ***

Old Nancy's blind. Born that way. But she's made the trip through the holler enough times to know every step on the trail. M'dad slaps the reins on Old Nancy's rump, then clicks twice with his tongue inside his cheek to get her movin'. Her milky eyes roll in their sockets, searchin' left, right—up and down—and her ears flick to and fro, listenin' for the sound of the wagon wheels switchin' from gravel to dirt as we roll through the barnyard. M'dad gives her a "Yahh!" and Old Nancy whinnies back. And just like that, she picks up her pace and we're headed out across the field towards the woods.

Me, Jack, and Jerry lay low in the back of the wagon, holdin' down the bottles to keep 'em from clankin'. The wagon wheels get quiet when we hit the rain-soaked leaves at the trail head. I peek out from under Old Nancy's blanket and see Grandmother's scarecrows standin' in the field, wearin' Grampa's clothes. Their tree-limb bodies are bent crooked like old Grampa, too. Hunched over in his old coveralls, soakin' wet in the night rain, the scarecrows watch us pass.

Before we know it, we're up into the woods where the scarecrows cain't see us, where Grandmother says her land ends and the Devil's begins. Me, Jack, and Jerry huddle close under Old Nancy's blanket in the back of the wagon tryin' to stay warm. And wasn't we wishin' for snow instead of a cold November rain stingin' our faces and freezin' our hair 'til it hangs stiff from our heads like icicles on the eaves of the barn in January.

The straw stuffed between the empty bottles keeps 'em from clankin' against each other and bustin'—and keeps 'em quiet, too, when we get deep into the woods. I rake a pile of straw around our feet to keep 'em warm. The rain's fallin' steady and kickin' up the dry smell of the barn when it hits the straw.

Jerry's about to nod off, squeezed tight between me and Jack. Grandmother says Jerry's got the angel face of his mother when he's sleepin'. "And the eyes of his devil father when he's awake," Mother throws in, always givin' little Jerry a pinch on the cheek and a wink when she says it.

Halfway up the ridge, the rain slows to a mist and the moon comes out. It's certain to be near midnight, and now Jack's noddin' off. I start to nudge him, like I do when I see him fallin' asleep in school, but then I think better of it. If I let him sleep now, I can take my share of winks on the way back home, while him and Jerry tends to the bottles.

I stick my head out from under the blanket, and I see M'dad sittin' up on the wagon seat. From behind he looks like Uncle Elvy, but I can tell it ain't, 'cause Uncle Elvy's missin' part of his right ear from when Old Nancy bit him. M'dad's ears are stickin' out from the sides of his stockin' cap, and even in the dark of night I can see his red curls hangin' wet and frozen on his shoulders.

The moon shines off M'dad's rain slicker, and for a moment it looks like there's a big white hole in his back and I can see clean through him, like he's hollow. But the wagon moves and

the moon shifts, and the hole in M'dad's back fills up, solid black again like wet tar.

I'm feelin' miserable cold and tryin' to keep Jerry and Jack warm under the blanket, when the wagon wheel hits the big rock we always hit, stickin' up in the mud. The wagon jerks to a stop and Old Nancy snorts. M'dad slaps the reins and shouts low, "Git up! Git up!" Old Nancy tries, but the rock is too big for us to go over, and we roll back a few feet on the trail. The bottles in the back of the wagon start clankin' against each other, and M'dad gives me the look over his shoulder. "Watch the feckin' bottles, Landy, or I'll take yer ass to the smoke shed when we git back."

I move quick to stuff more straw between the bottles, 'cause me, Jack, and Jerry think the smoke shed's the worst place in the world, and M'dad likes it that way. It don't take much to get M'dad pissed off enough to send us there, especially when he's drinkin' the shine. We'd be cryin', beggin' him, "Please, M'dad. We won't do it again." But for the life of us, we cain't ever figure out what it was we done. And when he lashes us with a hand full of willow switches, they crack like a whip, and with a dull swoosh they wrap around our legs 'til they raise blood and welts. It's the worst pain we ever know'd.

But for me, the worst part of the smoke shed is the scent of the smoked boar swingin' overhead. The smell of it fills my nose and moves quick to my stomach. And Mother wants to know why none of us boys, me, Jack, nor Jerry, likes the smoked meat when Grandmother cuts it down and brings it to the table. "It gets stuck in me throat," I says. Like a lump of somethin' I cain't never spit out.

In the back of the wagon, I scootch closer to the bottles to hold 'em steady. M'dad yells, "Yahh! Git!" and gives Old Nancy another hard snap with the reins. Even Old Nancy knows how M'dad can get when nothin' but a few miles stands between him and his shine. If no bottles gets broken and we have a good fill, we can all head straight to our beds when we get home, instead of headin' to the smoke shed.

M'dad pulls the reins to the left and Old Nancy finds her footin'. The wagon rolls over the rock, and down the hill we go in no time. And even though we counted the bottles back in the barn, I start countin' 'em again, tryin' to figure out how long it'll take us to fill 'em.

"One, two, three...," six rows of bottles across the back of the wagon. "One, two, three...," five rows of bottles deep. That's thirty bottles. An even number, thanks, God. An odd number and that'd be all it'd take to give M'dad reason to fill that extra bottle for himself, to drink it on the way back to the farm. It'll take at least two hours to fill thirty bottles. And if we fill 'em fast enough, M'dad might not take that strap to us and tell us, "Work faster, you lazy sons-o-bitches!"

Old Nancy's counted her steps from the barn, like I've counted the bottles, and knows exactly when to stop the wagon at the bottom of the hill. Jack and Jerry's heads raise up and their eyes open with a start when they feel the wagon stop. We're deep into the holler, and the rain's stopped a fallin'. I look out from under the blanket and see part of the old tin roof of the stillhouse on the other side of the hill. It's overgrown with shrubs and vines so thick, if I didn't know exactly where to look, I couldn't never find it.

"That's the way it's supposed to be," M'dad would growl when asked. "And if you ever tell a soul where it is, I'll beat all of you within an inch of your life!"

Knowin' how bad it feels to get the switch in the smoke shed, and how close I think I am to the end of my life when a good lashin' keeps me sleepin' on my stomach for a week, I shut my mouth and vow to never tell a soul. And Jack and Jerry, and even Mother, knows to never tell, too.

M'dad stops the wagon just outside the door of the stillhouse and hops down to walk Old Nancy around, turnin' her to face back up towards the hill. I slide the gate off the back of the wagon and me, Jack, and Jerry starts unloadin' the bottles. We all three got that dead tired look on our faces. We're hopin' M'dad will be in the mood to fill 'em and load 'em fast and get back to the farm, so we can roll into our beds before the rooster starts crowin'.

I look over and see M'dad reach under the wagon seat and pull out an empty bottle. Number thirty-one. And I'm wishin'

Uncle Elvy hadn't broken his leg fallin' outta the hay loft, so's he'd be here instead of us.

Jerry's in the back of the wagon so's he can hand the empty bottles down to me and Jack. The moon's reflectin' off the bottles at our feet, and it's like a dozen bright eyes lookin' back up at us. We carry all the bottles into the stillhouse, while M'dad climbs to the top of the ridge, carryin' bottle thirty-one under his arm. I see him up on top of the hill through the trees, near where Grandmother says the Devil's land begins. He looks up at the moon, then looks into the woods and stands perfect still with his head cocked, just so, to listen. After he's satisfied nobody's followed us, he climbs back down the hill with his bottle still tucked under his arm, and comes inside the stillhouse where me, Jack, and Jerry are waitin'.

*** *** ***

We know to keep quiet as a field mouse. M'dad closes the stillhouse door behind him and crouches down, so he don't crack his head on the beams. It's all pitch black 'til we hear the match strike. M'dad's weathered face lights up behind the flame. When he puts the match to the wick in the lamp, our shadows stretch across the walls and the ceilin', bendin' our bodies like the scarecrows in the field.

I see the outline of the copper tub in the corner, sittin' up on bricks for legs. A pinched coil of copper tube sticks out the side of the tub and feeds its way into the top of the oak barrel Grandmother used to use to catch rainwater out beside the house. Near the bottom of the oak barrel, another copper tube sticks out from the side and coils up where it hooks on a rusty nail in the wall. Me, Jack, and Jerry sit on an old tree stump and wait for M'dad to give us the okay to start fillin' the bottles with shine.

M'dad adjusts the light from the lamp and the shadow of the still stretches up the wall, and for a moment it looks like one of the old wild boars that Uncle Elvy hunts in the woods. I start feelin' sick thinkin' 'bout the dried blood behind the smoke shed where the dogs wait for slaughter scraps.

M'dad walks over to the still with bottle thirty-one in his hand. Me, Jack, and Jerry watch as he unhooks the coil from the nail and feeds it into the lip of the bottle, so the shine can start flowin'. M'dad starts talkin' to the copper pot, smilin' like when he's talkin' up Mother after a night of drinkin' and dancin' to Uncle Elvy's fiddle. "Yer a beautiful sight," he says to the copper pot. "Just beautiful."

Me, Jack, and Jerry are sittin' on the stump in the shadows, watchin' and listenin' as M'dad talks to the still like we ain't even there. And I'm wishin' we wasn't.

M'dad fills bottle thirty-one first and says, "Git yourselves busy with the rest of 'em." We jump to it fast, slidin' the bottles over to the still. I put the coil down and let the shine drip into the first bottle.

"I'll be watchin'," says M'dad, "so no feckin' around and spillin' it."

He disappears through the stillhouse door with his bottle of shine in his hand, and I know the rest of the work will be up to us. I hold tight to the coil, and Jack and Jerry squat down to watch the shine drip slow into the bottom of the first bottle.

More than an hour's passed and the rain starts up again, only harder than before, rattlin' on the tin roof. We hear Old Nancy outside snortin' and a stompin' her hooves for attention. She don't like the rain, and I don't blame 'er. I hand bottle number twenty-one to Jack and says, "Put the blanket on Old Nancy when you load this one in the wagon." A few minutes later when Jack comes back in, he's danglin' an empty bottle from two fingers.

"Landy," says Jack in a whisper, "M'dad's passed out in the back of the wagon under Old Nancy's blanket. Should we fill his bottle again?"

"Forget it," I says. "Don't wake him. Leave him there. Maybe he'll drown in the rain."

Jerry starts to laugh at that and gets Jack to laughin', too. Jack says, "It'd be good enough for him if he did drown."

"Ya think it's funny, do ya, Jack?" I says. "Do ya, Jerry? It won't be so funny if M'dad wakes up and finds you laughin' and carryin' on, and not fillin' up the bottles."

That shuts up Jerry and Jack both, 'cause there's nothin' M'dad takes more serious than his shine, and they know it. And if he sobers up to the sound of us laughin', we're sure to get it quick and without a warnin'.

The rest of the bottles fill fast, with M'dad out to the world. We're careful not to wake him when we fill bottle number thirty and load it into the back of the wagon where M'dad's layin', surrounded by bottles of shine. The rain's still comin' down and Old Nancy's anxious to go. I run back to the stillhouse to snuff the light and lock the door. With M'dad out cold, I hop into the wagon seat and take the reins to Old Nancy.

*** *** ***

The moon's gone behind the night clouds, and I cain't see more than a few yards in front of Old Nancy's nose. The lower limbs of the bare trees reach out over the trail like the arms of the scarecrows in the field. I think of Grandmother sittin' in her rockin' chair tellin' me, Jack, and Jerry 'bout the Devil in the holler grabbin' us, wrappin' his boney arms around us and whiskin' us away to his fiery pit. I holler, "Git," and snap the reins to get Old Nancy goin'. She takes off with a start, rattlin' the bottles in the back of the wagon.

"Hold them damn bottles," I whisper loud to Jack and Jerry behind me. "Not a one of 'em better be busted when we get back, or you'll get yours from me and M'dad. Count on it."

Old Nancy's anxious to get back to the warm barn and outta the rain. She's counted her steps and halfway up the trail she tries to pick up her pace, but I slow her down to keep the bottles from knockin'. "Whoa-hoa," I says, and she slows down to take the sharp turn in the path headin' up the last hill.

The cold rain makes the leaves coverin' the trail slick, and Old Nancy loses her footin' and tenses up in the reins. We hit that same rock we had trouble with comin' into the woods, and the wagon slides off to the side of the trail. The front wheel of the wagon gets lodged against the rock, and Old Nancy starts up with a whinny, 'cause that blasted rock is keepin' her from her warm barn and bucket of oats.

I slap the reins on her rump and holler, "Yahh! Git!" But Old Nancy cain't get her footin' enough to pull the wagon over the rock. Her eyes are rollin' in their sockets, and she lets out a long snort. We're both tryin' to get over that rock, and I know she's just as mad as me. I try to back Old Nancy outta the mud and away from the rock, but no matter which way I guide her, the wagon keeps slidin' back into the same rut on the trail.

Jack and Jerry are huddled in the back of the wagon, holdin' tight to the bottles to keep 'em from clankin'. M'dad's still layin' in the straw, dead to the world.

"Jack," I says. "Git up here and take the reins whilst I hop down and push."

Jack steps over M'dad and scurries up to the front of the

wagon and plops down in the seat beside me. I pass the reins to Jack and says, "Hold 'em tight. And give Old Nancy a lashin' when I holler."

I jump from the wagon and sink to my ankles in the mud. I try to lift my right leg out and nearly lose my boot. Jerry's sittin' in the back of the wagon holdin' tight to the bottles, careful not to wake M'dad sprawled out in the rain-soaked straw.

I make my way through the mud to the rear of the wagon and press my back to the gate and push. I holler, "Git," and Jack hollers, "Yahh!" and cracks the reins on Old Nancy's rump. Old Nancy raises her head and pulls the wagon forward 'til the wheel stops against the rock. "Git!" I holler louder, and Jack yells, "Yah!" and cracks the reins again. But no matter how hard Old Nancy tries, and no matter how hard I push, the wagon won't budge.

"Jack," I says, "Jump down and help me push. Let Old Nancy pull it on her own. She knows what to do."

Jack wraps the reins around the boot rest and jumps down in the mud to help me. All the while, Jerry's holdin' tight to the bottles in the back of the wagon to keep 'em from clankin'. The moon's doin' its best to break from the clouds, but the rain keeps comin' down in a fine mist.

Poor Jerry's soaked to the bone. He pulls the sleeves of his shirt down over his hands to keep 'em warm. It's the shirt I passed down to Jack when I outgrew it, and then Jack passed it down to Jerry. There weren't much left of it to speak of, all worn and thin, and soaked clean through, clingin' to Jerry like a loose layer of skin.

M'dad's still curled up in his rain slicker, huggin' a bottle in the back of the wagon. I'm pushin' with all my might on the back of the wagon gate, with my feet sinkin' deeper in the mud. All the while, I'm wishin' M'dad would never wake up, like I wish every time he hits the bottle. But he always wakes, and that's what keeps me pushin' harder and hollerin' at Old Nancy, "Yahh! Git up!"

Old Nancy's tryin', but she cain't get over that rock. I'm grittin' my teeth, gettin' sorer by the minute, when I look over the back of the gate into the wagon and see little Jerry doin' all he can to hold them bottles in place, while M'dad's just layin' in the back of the wagon sleepin' off the shine.

"Hold on, Jerry," I says. "We almost got it!"

With me and Jack pushin' and Old Nancy pullin', the wagon's rockin' somethin' fierce, 'til even M'dad's limp body starts rockin' with it. One more big push and M'dad slides down the back of the wagon with a crash into the bottles. Two bottles bust clean open and shine starts pourin' out through the gate, soakin' me from shoulders to boots.

"No!" I shout. "No! Jerry, hold tight to the bottles."

The shine drips out of the wagon gate and soaks my head. My eyes start to burn. We're all sure to get the switch now. Maybe worse!

The moon peeks out over the top of the trees. The shine keeps a drippin' and the rain keeps a fallin'. I look up and I see Old Nancy rearin' her head back and pullin' with all she's got. Her hot breath shoots from her nose into the cold night air and fades. Old Nancy's tryin', but she still cain't get enough footin' to pull the wagon over that rock. I'm pushin' so hard my legs start to wobble so's I cain't control 'em.

"Jerry," I says, "Grab some straw and toss it under the wheels whilst me and Jack push. Hurry, Jerry! Hurry!"

Jerry lets loose of the last of the bottles he's holdin' and starts throwin' straw over the side of the wagon. The bottles slide towards the gate and stop quick with a clatter when they reach M'dad layin' in the middle of the broken glass, smellin' to high heaven like the shine. The rain's beatin' down on us so hard now, I can hardly see. My hair's drippin' wet, clingin' to my face.

Through the mud and the shine burnin' my eyes, I can see Jerry tossin' straw over the side of the wagon just as fast as he can. His arms are small in the loose sleeves of my old shirt, like the boneless arms of Grandmother's scarecrows fightin' in a mad rage against the wind in a storm. But Jerry don't give up. He keeps tossin' the straw over the side of the wagon, 'til there's nothin' left but little whisps of straw around M'dad's limp body.

"Jump down, Jerry," I says. "Shove the straw under the wheels."

Jerry jumps over the side of the wagon and lands deep in the mud. He tries to take a first step, but the mud is so thick it holds tight to his feet like a spoon standin' straight up in a pot of cold oatmeal. Jerry tugs again, and on the third try he breaks free, leavin' his boot in the mud. His wool sock dangles from his foot, but with a quick tug, Jerry slips the sock up his leg and pulls his boot free.

"Hurry, Jerry," I says. "If another bottle breaks and M'dad wakes up, we're sure as dead."

Jerry gathers a bundle of straw in his arms and starts tossin' it under the wheels.

"Jack, you have to push harder," I says. "Push to the left. Now forward!"

I'm pushin' so hard I feel the gate start to slide loose. I grab tight and hold it in place to keep what's left of the shine and M'dad from spillin' out the back of the wagon. I'm pushin' and Jack's pushin', and we've almost got it.

"Jerry," I says. "Throw more straw under the wheel. We're almost there. More straw!"

The last of the bottles at the head of the wagon start slidin' towards the gate, clankin' against each other around M'dad. I'm thinkin' so hard about keepin' those bottles from breakin' and how we're gonna get the switch for sure, I'm not watchin' little Jerry like I should. He's slippin' every step he takes, but he manages to crawl under the wagon between me and Jack as we're pushin' and Old Nancy's pullin'. The sleeves of my old shirt keep slidin' over Jerry's little hands, gettin' in his way as he tosses straw under the wheel.

"Pull up your sleeves, Jerry," I says. "Your sleeves. Pull 'em up!"

But little Jerry's workin' as hard as any of us, tossin' straw under the wheels, and he won't stop for nothin'. Old Nancy keeps a pullin' and a snortin', and one last push from me and Jack is all it takes for the wagon to lurch forward over the rock.

The moon pulls the clouds aside and shines bright as a lantern across the wagon. Old Nancy's milky eyes start rollin' in their sockets, strainin' to see what's goin' on behind her. In the bright white light of the moon, as the wagon rolls up and over the rock, I see little Jerry slip in the mud and fall under the wheel, caught by his shirt sleeve. A horrible scream rips open the night.

"Holy God!" I holler. "Jerry! Jerry! Jack, git Jerry. He's under the wheel. Git Jerry!"

I push hard against the gate with my shoulder to keep the wagon from rollin' back, and Jack scrambles under the wagon to reach Jerry.

"Whoa, Old Nancy!" I yell, "Whoa!"

"Help me, Landy!" Jerry screams, "Help me!"

But I cain't do a thing or else the gate on the wagon will come loose and all the shine will spill out the back, and then wouldn't we all get it. We'd get it for sure.

Jerry's screams drift out from under the wagon and up into the treetops. With no leaves on the trees to hold back the pitiful noise, Jerry's voice just keeps travelin' deep into the empty woods, until I can hear it echo across the ravine and travel back to us again, like there's another Jerry screamin' from the Devil's land on the other side of the ridge.

Jack's pullin' on Jerry's trousers, tryin' to pull him free from the wheel, but Jack's slippin' in the mud and cain't get a hold of little Jerry. I'm still pushin' my shoulder to the gate when the wheel rolls forward over little Jerry's neck. And that's all Old Nancy needs to pull the wagon up onto the rock and down the other side.

I watch as Jerry's face disappears into the mud and straw under the weight of the wheel, and his scream is silenced.

"M'dad!" I holler. "The wagon! M'dad! Jerry's stuck under the wagon. Wake up! M'dad! Wake up! Jack, wake him up! Shake him!"

Jack scampers from under the wagon and climbs into the back to wake M'dad.

"He's dead to the world, Landy," says Jack. "I cain't wake him. He's dead to the world."

Tears and mud are stingin' my eyes. I choke on my own screams.

"Wake him, Jack! Kick him! Kick him!"

I'm wishin' M'dad really was dead to the world. Dead to us all. Maybe then we could all just farm the land proper, with the help of Uncle Elvy and Mother, and not have to live on the bad money of M'dad's shine. Maybe then we could buy nice things, like a fancy glass pin for mother's winter coat, so she could walk proud into church. And Grandmother could head right over to Ruth's grocer and pay up what we owe 'em—with enough left over to buy a loaf of bread and a pound of cheese sliced so thin you could see daylight through it. And wouldn't we all be happier, if only M'dad were dead to us all.

Little Jerry's half gone under the mud and he's not movin'. I let loose of the wagon gate and the bottles of shine come crashin' out the back. M'dad rolls out into the mud behind 'em. I crawl under the wagon and scoot over to little Jerry. I rip away my old shirt from his body and pull him free from the mud, hollerin' all the while.

"Jerry! Jerry, Jerry git up. Git up, Jerry!"

But the way little Jerry's head rolls to the side and back, I can tell that he's already gone from this world. I wipe the mud and straw from his face, holdin' him as close as I can, sittin' there under the wagon rockin' him in my arms. Over and over I say his name.

"Jerry! Jerry!" I cry, wantin' him to answer. But down inside I know that final dreadful scream of his would be the last I hear from him.

"Jerry! Jerrrry!"

I look up and Jack's standin' beside M'dad passed out in the mud, watchin' me rock back and forth with Jerry in my arms. All the while I'm wonderin' how I'm gonna tell Mother that her baby Jerry's neck was broke under the wheel of the wagon, and how I'm to blame, 'cause I let him crawl beneath it to shove straw under the wheel. "Why'd I let you crawl under the wagon, Jerry? Why didn't I keep you safe in the back with M'dad and the shine? Why didn't I, Jerry? Why didn't I?"

My ears are full of silence. I hear nothin'. I hear nothin'. Then a long, dark sob snakes from deep inside my chest and coils into the air above me. It echoes back across the ridge to the Devil's land, like little Jerry's screams. Old Nancy whinnies with a high pitch. Her head bobs up and back as she prances in place and takes her hooves to the mud, ready to take off into the woods. Her eyes roll back and her ears strain toward her tail, as she's tryin' to figure out what's goin' on behind her. Jack grabs the reins and calms her down. "Whoa, Old Nancy. Whoa."

The rain starts up again and the moon slips behind the November sky.

*** *** ***

When the wagon clears the woods and reaches the bottom of the hill near the pasture, Grandmother's standin' in the field with the scarecrows, waitin' for the wagon and knowin' something's wrong. She's wringin' her hands, wailin' into the night sky, pacin' in circles, and lookin' back into the woods over her shoulder. Old Nancy smells how Grandmother's afraid and lets out a whinny that curls her lip and starts her eyes to rollin' in their sockets. She stiffens up and don't want to move.

"H-ya!" I yells to Old Nancy, and slap the reins across her back. "H-ya!"

But Old Nancy won't move any closer to Grandmother. And that's when Grandmother raises her hand to the moon and lets out a cry that strips the dark out of the sky. Old Nancy rears up on her hind legs, and the moon slides out from behind the clouds, casting a silver glow over Grandmother and the scarecrows in the field. I slap the reins down hard on Old Nancy's rump, and the wagon bolts into the clearin', past Grandmother, past the scarecrows, and straight to the barn, with me tryin' to control her.

I'm not the one to tell Mother that her baby, Jerry, is dead. Mother hears Grandmother wailin', and Old Nancy whinnyin', and she runs out to the barn to see what's the commotion. Old Nancy's eyes are rollin' blind in their sockets, strainin' to see M'dad laid out in the back of the wagon and Jack holdin' little Jerry in his arms.

There's noise, high-pitched and wailin', when Mother and Grandmother rush into the barn. Mother sees Jack holdin' little Jerry. She sees me at the reins and M'dad passed out in the wagon. And then I cain't hear a thing, except my heart thumpin' inside my chest and blood poundin' in my ears. I cain't hear a thing.

I jump into the back of the wagon where Jack's holdin' little Jerry and M'dad's still passed out with his bottle. I take little Jerry from Jack's arms and I hold him close to my chest. I see Mother and Grandmother rush to the back of the wagon. I see their mouths movin', and their hands tearin' at their faces and pullin' on their hair. I cain't hear 'em, but I can feel their screams inside me. Their arms reach into the wagon and drag little Jerry away from me, not knowin' which end of him to touch, to hold first. Their hands grab at him, clutchin' frantic like he's about to float away, tearin' at his clothes to pull him closer.

Mother pushes Jerry's wet hair back out of his cold, blue face and clears the mud from his eyes. I watch their faces. First Mother, then Grandmother. I see their lips movin', but I cain't hear a thing they're sayin'. My ears are full, like I'm under water. My head begins to pound with the rush of blood drainin' from my heart. I stand in the wagon, holdin' Old Nancy's reins. Her eyes roll, and her ears point straight back tryin' to hear what's happen' in the wagon behind her. In a final swift move, Mother's got little Jerry clutched in her arms, runnin' to the house with Grandmother and Jack followin' behind her.

My head. My head feels like it's gonna burst. I'm thinkin' I'm near as an inch to the end of my life. The pain's worse than any beatin' I ever got from M'dad. Old Nancy's still rollin' her eyes back, strugglin' to see what's what. My chest and my head are gonna burst open. I drop to my knees in the back of the wagon. M'dad's layin' there with his bottle, passed out, lookin' like he's asleep without a care, like he cain't feel nothin' at all. He cain't feel nothin'. And all I want is to feel nothin', too. I want to feel nothin', like M'dad.

I pull the bottle from M'dad's hands and pop the cork. My head is poundin'. I cain't hear. I put the bottle to my lips and tip it back to take a long swig. I taste my tears, salty on the lip of the bottle, mixin' with the shine. I swallow hard and fast in big gulps, like I'm drinkin' water on a hot day. It burns. My throat burns and shine comes up through my nose. It feels like I swallowed hot coals. I spit it out. My ears open up, like I surfaced on the pond, and I can suddenly hear again. But all I can hear is the bottomed-out sound of me cryin' and wailin'.

"Jerry! Jerry!"

The burn moves to my stomach, but it don't burn the pain away. I tip the bottle back and drink again, longer this time, tryin' to wash away the burn. I start to feel sick, but I cain't put the bottle down. I want to feel nothin', like M'dad feels nothin'. I drink again. I drink again 'til the burn washes clean inside me, and I fall dizzy into the back of the wagon next to M'dad.

I begin to feel it. The nothin'. I begin to feel the nothin', like M'dad. I think about poor, dead little Jerry. I tip the bottle again and start to feel more of nothin'. I think of Jack and Grandmother. My eyes close and open heavy. I think of Mother and the pin I want to buy her, so she can walk proud into church. I think of the bread, and cheese sliced so thin I can see daylight through it. I take another swallow of the shine, and I cain't hear nothin' again.

My eyes close. I feel myself sinkin' back into the wagon next to M'dad. One last time I open my eyes, and I see Old Nancy's blind white eyes lookin' back at me, bulgin' in their sockets. The burn from the shine begins to fade, and my screams sink deep into my chest.

"Jerry! Jerry!"

I'm feelin' more of nothin'. More of what M'dad feels. I'm feelin' nothin'. And just before my eyes close and the shine takes me under, I look through the open door of the barn and watch a dark mist move across the moon.

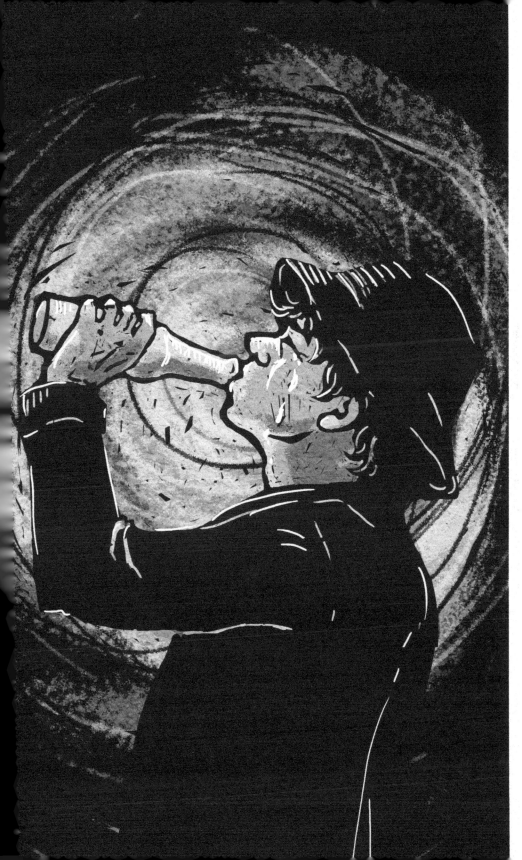

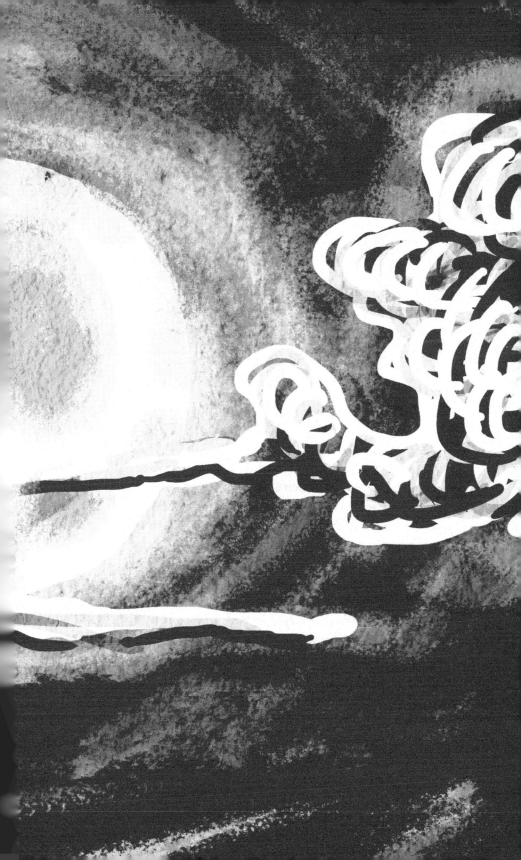

Acknowledgements

Many thanks to my early readers, dear friends, and listeners of this work, without whom this story might never have seen the light of day. You gave me confidence in my work and the courage to share it.

Joanie Bennett, your willingness to steep yourself in the details and become emotionally invested in the characters proved to me that others are hungry to read the types of stories I enjoy writing. Your love for this tale runs as deep as mine.

Jeremy Denzer, your ability to put up with my eccentricities and accept them as normal, everyday behavior says more about you than it does about me. It is my fortune to feel your love.

Margie Ferro, your enthusiastic and honest response upon your first reading was such a tremendous gift. You understood exactly what I was trying to achieve. I wasn't sure I had the talent to convey that to the reader, but you convinced me otherwise.

Craig Moodie, your early input and advice was invaluable. Your willingness to listen to my earliest recordings of Landy and let him tell the story—not me—set me on the correct path. Your instinct as a storyteller is spot on!

Natalia Slattery, you have an amazing gift! Thank you for so lovingly and accurately carving out these characters and giving them visual life.

Therese...*where do I even begin?*

About the author

Rick Hall grew up in a small farming community on the prairie of central Illinois. The son of a father with southern roots and a homemaker mother born and raised in central Illinois, he is the youngest of 21 children and comes from a long lineage of farmers. His unique upbringing has shaped his perspective on everything from his relationship with nature to the way he connects with people and nurtures relationships—all of which continue to influence his storytelling and writing.

About the artist

Natalia Slattery is an artist and illustrator whose work highlights small moments of intimacy. Born and raised in Massachusetts, Natalia now resides in New York City. A multi-disciplinary artist at heart, Natalia draws techniques from printmaking, collage, and painting in her work, and loves connecting with students in her teaching practice. To learn more about her work, visit nataliaslattery.com or @adas_estate on Instagram.